HIDDEN WARRIORS

A powerful djinn called Nadakhan is close to conquering Ninjago world with his Sky Pirates. Will the Spinjitzu Masters be able to thwart his plans? Look at the scene and find the five ninja preparing for attack.

CAPTURED!

Nadakhan has imprisoned Kai in his magical blade. Which other ninja have been trapped in the sword prison as well? Use the clues in the white box to draw straight lines connecting the sets of symbols. The new prisoners are the ones crossed through by the lines you have drawn.

SABOTAGE!

The Sky Pirates want to capture Nya and Jay. Spoil their plans by stopping Nadakhan's ship from taking off! Replace the working parts of the Raid Zeppelin with broken ones by circling the parts in the picture.

BROKEN PARTS

DOUBLE ZANE

Nya and Jay escaped from prison and ended up in a lighthouse where they found Echo Zane. Help the ninja turn the robot on by connecting the cables to complete the circuits. Each one must have the same symbol on either end.

After Nya was captured by Nadakhan, and almost all of the ninja were imprisoned in the djinn's sword, only Jay was left to face the Sky Pirates. But he didn't have to do it all by himself ...

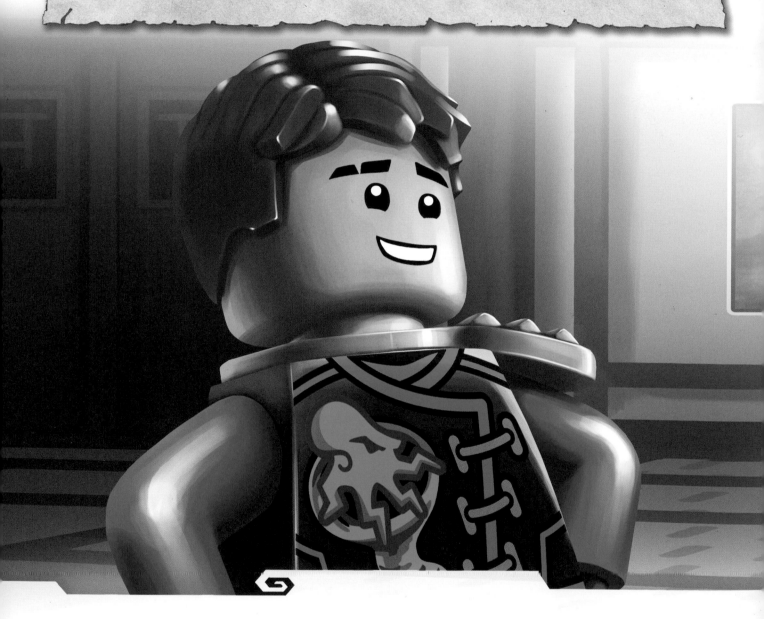

Look at the photo of the new team Jay has put together. Match each member to their description beneath the photo.

a. A fearsome bounty hunter who wears an eyepatch.

b. He protects the law working at the police department in Ninjago City.

c. He and Zane are twins ... that is, if robots can be twins.

d. Look out for her bright kimono!

e. His brown belt actually says nothing about his lack of fighting skills.

f. He is missing an arm, a leg and an eye - but he's still better than most pirate captains!

BACK IN ACTION

Searching for his friends in Nadakhan's sword was an adventure and a half! But eventually, Jay found and freed Kai, Cole, Lloyd, Zane, Master Wu and Misako.

The ninja escaped the djinn prison. Can you spot ten differences between the two pictures?

"I'm sure I saw him go in there," insisted Jay.

Kai looked at the restaurant on the corner. Through the windows, he could see it was full of people enjoying their dinner.

"I hope you're right," he said. "Those doubles of us running around robbing and looting have made us wanted men."

"Don't worry," said Jay, as he crossed the street. "I used to eat here all the time, back when you insisted on cooking for the team. Anything to avoid that! The manager will be happy to see us."

"OK, I ... hey! What's wrong with my cooking?" demanded Kai.

"Well, the next time the Skeleton Army invades, we're having you cater," Jay said, smiling.

"Oh, come on," protested Kai.

"Peanut butter stew," said Jay, as they entered the restaurant.

"But ..."

"Swamp eel surprise."

"Well, I ..."

"Grilled fangfish in rockslide bat sauce with Brussels sprouts."

When the manager saw Jay, his eyes widened.

"What are you doing back here?" he demanded. "I told you to leave. I just saw you go into the kitchen. You should have gone out the back door!"

"That wasn't me," answered Jay. "I ..."

"Went out the back door and in the front door," Kai cut in. "I love noodles. Let's see how they make them, Jay."

The two ninja rushed through the swinging doors into the kitchen. An instant later, the manager saw Jay come back through the same door.

"I thought you were getting noodles?" he said.

"In this dump?" said evil Jay. "I wouldn't feed this slop to a Serpentine. Let's see what I can do to improve this place."

Laughing, the evil ninja went back into the kitchen. A minute later, the front door opened and Jay and Kai walked in.

The manager stalked over to them. "It isn't slop!" he bellowed at Jay. "You're going to 'improve' it? Why, you ..."

"Uh-oh," said Kai. "While we were searching the alley out back, he must have come back in here."

The two ninja rushed into the kitchen. The whole place was full of steam.

"I can't see anything," said Jay. "Kai, you go that way."

Kai plunged into the steamy kitchen. He navigated around counters and kitchen workers until he reached the back of the room. That's when he spotted Jay.

"I haven't found your double," said Kai.

"Sure you have!" said evil Jay, tossing a lightning bolt that Kai just managed to duck.

"Jay, he's back here!" yelled Kai.

"Not for long," said evil Jay. He disappeared into the clouds of steam, but not before the real Jay spotted him. Kai saw one Jay duck into a supply cupboard and the other one go in after him. The door shut behind them. A moment later, it opened again and Jay came out ... again.

"There must have been a secret exit in there," said the mystery Jay. "When I went in, he was gone. Look for yourself."

Keeping an eye on Jay, Kai leaned into the cupboard. He didn't see evil Jay come up behind him. The double shoved Kai inside the cupboard, then slammed the door and locked it.

Kai almost stumbled over Jay, who was on the floor in a potato sack. Kai swiftly freed him.

"I'll fry the lock," said Jay, "and then let's get that guy."

The two ninja burst out of the cupboard and into the kitchen, which now resembled an exploded noodle factory. Noodles were clinging to the walls and ceiling. Jay's double had been busy.

"You! You!" sputtered the manager, rushing up to them. "Look what you did to my kitchen!"

"Which way did I go after I was done?" asked Jay.

"Huh?" replied the manager. "Listen, if this is about that time last month when the Ninja Noodle Special came out crunchy, I can always …"

"Wait a minute," said Jay. "That's it!"

"What's it?" said Kai.

"Bad food! Maybe that's the answer."

"What do you mean, bad food?" sputtered the manager. "Why, this is one of the best …"

"Not anymore," said Jay. "I've got an idea. Listen, am I still here?"

"Of course you are!" snapped the manager. "You're right in front of me!"

"But is he anywhere else?" asked Kai.

"Go out front and check," Jay said to Kai. "I've got an idea."

Kai peered through the swinging door. Evil Jay was still in the restaurant, wandering around sampling everyone's food.

Meanwhile, Jay quickly told the manager his plan ...

The manager walked out into the dining area to make an announcement to his customers.

"May I have your attention, please!" he began. "Tonight, as a special treat we have a celebrity chef in the house. All of the food will be made by ... Kai!"

"That's right," said Jay. "And he's going to make some of his best dishes ... aren't you, Kai?"

"Uh ... right," said Kai. "We'll start with rancid stinkberries in moudly cheese ... followed by water rat and pondweed casserole ... and for dessert ..."

"Pickle-flavoured ice cream," added Jay.

Evil Jay looked horror-stricken. Then he vanished in a puff of smoke.

"What just happened?" asked Kai.

"He was defeated by the one power no one can overcome," answered Jay. "The thought of your disgusting cooking!"

A GREAT MESS

Dareth wants to fight Nadakhan, but first he needs to deal with the mess the ninja left after their morning training. Help him by matching the weapons into pairs. Which one only appears once?

THAT SINKING FEELING

THE SKY PIRATES HAVE BEEN PREYING ON SEASIDE TOWNS IN THEIR RAID ZEPPELIN.

TOWN OFF THE STERN ... I MEAN TOWN OFF THE BOW ... I MEAN, WHATEVER THAT POINTY THING UP FRONT IS!

ZANE IS CLOSING IN ON THE SKY PIRATES, BUT –

THE PIRATES HAVE A SECRET FLOATING BASE ... AND THEY DON'T LIKE VISITORS.

CATAPULT AWAY!

KA-KAMM

HOW INCONVENIENT.

UNINVITED GUESTS

Nadakhan wants to marry Nya and become even more powerful. The ninja plan to interrupt their wedding! Number the pieces in the correct order so that Lloyd and Cole can launch an attack.

LOOKING FOR VENOM

After losing the Spider Widow's venom in a fight with the Sky Pirates, the ninja have to get it back. Clancee wants to reveal the place where he hid the only weapon capable of destroying the djinn! Which line leads Zane to the vial of poison?

I DON'T KNOW ABOUT YOU, BUT I'VE HAD IT WITH THAT BIG-HEADED DJINN!

DESTINATION: TEMPLE

The ninja found the venom and now they can face Nadakhan! Help them cross the maze and reach the Djinn Temple. That's where Nadakhan is holding his new wife – Nya. Hurry, there's no time to lose!

START

FINISH

FINAL SHOWDOWN

Nadakhan made a wish and copies of the djinn surrounded the ninja! But which one is the original Nadakhan? To find out, look at the pictures and mark the djinn who has exactly the same coloured symbols next to him as the box on the opposite page.

a

b

c

d

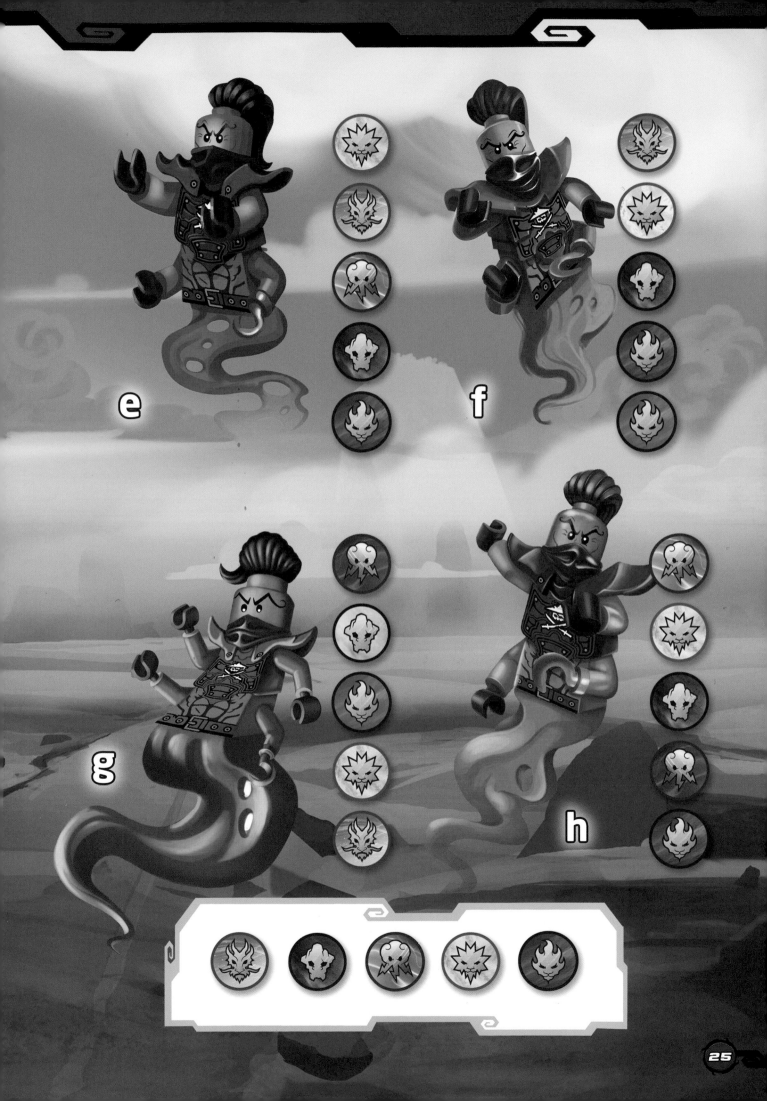

DJINN AT GUNPOINT

Now Flintlocke has joined the ninja! This rebellious pirate can hit Nadakhan with a poisoned dart with his eyes closed! Try your luck – close your eyes and find out if you can place the tip of your pen at the centre of the target.

HIDDEN LAMP

Nadakhan was defeated and the djinn's lamp was hidden on a large barge full of rubbish! Look at the lamp that Clouse's ghost is thinking about and find it in the pile before he does.

PIRATE QUIZ

Now that Ninjago world is safe again, it's time to check what you remember about the ninja and their struggle with Nadakhan and his Sky Pirates. Read the questions and choose the right answers.

1. Nadakhan wanted to turn Ninjago Island into:
   a. Nadanjago
   b. Eldorado
   c. Djinnjago

2. Which ninja weren't imprisoned in Nadakhan's sword?
   a. Zane and Jay
   b. Nya and Zane
   c. Nya and Jay

3. Which ship belonged to the Sky Pirates?
   a. *Destiny's Bounty*
   b. *Raid Zeppelin*
   c. *Misfortune's Keep*

4. Who freed the prisoners from Nadakhan's sword?
   a. Dareth
   b. Ronin
   c. Jay

5. Who wasn't part of the support team?
   a. Captain Soto
   b. Dareth
   c. Nya

6. Who did Nadakhan want to marry?
   a. Nya
   b. Skylor
   c. A djinn princess

7. What did Flintlocke use to defeat Nadakhan?
   a. Tiger Widow's venom
   b. Sabre-toothed Tiger's saliva
   c. Tiger Salamander's blood

ANSWERS

Pg. 1
HIDDEN WARRIORS

Pg. 2-3
CAPTURED!

Pg. 4-5
SABOTAGE!

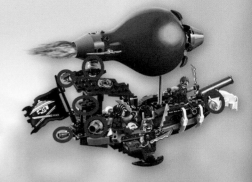

Pg. 7
DOUBLE ZANE

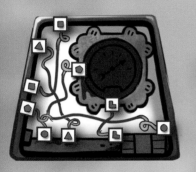

Pg. 8-9
SUPPORT TEAM

Pg. 10-11
BACK IN ACTION

Pg. 17
A GREAT MESS

Pg. 20
UNINVITED GUESTS

Pg. 21
LOOKING FOR VENOM

Pg. 22-23
DESTINATION: TEMPLE

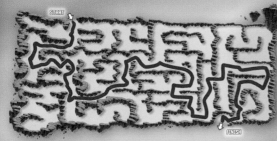

Pg. 24-25
FINAL SHOWDOWN

Pg. 27
HIDDEN LAMP

Pg. 28-29
PIRATE QUIZ: 1 – c, 2 – c, 3 – b, 4 – c, 5 – c, 6 – a, 7 – a.